Annie
the Detective
Fairy

By Daisy Meadows

ORCHARD

www.rainbowmagicbooks.co.uk

Annie
the Detective
Fairy

Join the **Rainbow Magic Reading Challenge!**

nd the story and collect your fairy points to climb the
Reading Rainbow at the back of the book.

This book is worth 5 points.

To Ella

Special thanks to Rachel Elliot

ORCHARD BOOKS

First published in Great Britain in 2019 by The Watts Publishing Group

3 5 7 9 10 8 6 4 2

© 2019 Rainbow Magic Limited.
© 2019 HIT Entertainment Limited.
Illustrations © Orchard Books 2019

HIT entertainment

A CIP catalogue record for this book is available from the British Library.

ISBN 978 1 40835 516 9

Printed and bound in Great Britain by CPI Group (UK) Ltd, Croydon, CR0 4YY

MIX
Paper from
responsible sources
FSC® C104740
www.fsc.org

The paper and board used in this book are made from wood from responsible sources

Orchard Books
An imprint of Hachette Children's Group
Part of The Watts Publishing Group Limited
Carmelite House, 50 Victoria Embankment, London EC4Y 0DZ

An Hachette UK Company
www.hachette.co.uk
www.hachettechildrens.co.uk

Jack Frost's Spell

Those brainy fairies make me cross.
One day Jack Frost will be their boss.
I'll solve each baffling mystery
And make each great discovery.

I'll steal their magic books away
And grow more crafty every day.
No clever-clogs in history
Will be as brilliant as me!

Contents

Chapter One: Midnight Stroll   9

Chapter Two: Hello Fairyland!   21

Chapter Three: The Mystery of the   33
Missing Toadstool

Chapter Four: Clients for Shivershock Bones   43

Chapter Five: The Pieces of the Puzzle   55

Chapter Six: Mystery Solved!   65

Chapter One
Midnight Stroll

SNUFFLE! SNORE! The Science Museum echoed with sleepy noises. It was the night of the big sleepover, and every gallery was filled with mums, dads, children and sleeping bags.

In the Discover Space gallery, only two children were still awake.

"I'm too excited to sleep," whispered Rachel Walker.

"Me too," said her best friend, Kirsty Tate. "After our magical adventures earlier, I keep expecting another fairy to pop up."

The girls were lying next to each other. There was just enough light in the gallery for them to exchange a happy smile. They loved sharing the wonderful secret that they were friends with the fairies.

"It's great that we helped Aisha and Orla find their magical notebooks,"

Rachel went on. "But Jack Frost still has the other two notebooks. Until we get them back, the Discovery Fairies won't be able to help, inspire or guide anyone."

Kirsty turned on to her side and propped herself up on her elbow.

"I'm sure we'll get the chance to help Annie and Elsie soon," she said.

The Ice Lord and his naughty goblins had been causing trouble again. They had stolen the magical notebooks that belonged to the Discovery Fairies. Rachel and Kirsty had visited Mission Control in Fairyland, where the Discovery Fairies watched over humans and fairies. Without their notebooks, they weren't able to do their jobs.

"Shall we go for a walk around the museum?" Rachel suggested. "It might

tire us out enough to be able to sleep."

"Great idea," said Kirsty. "We can choose which gallery we want to visit tomorrow."

Rachel took a couple of apples out of her rucksack.

"Midnight feast," she said, grinning. "Come on."

The girls picked up their torches and tiptoed past the rows of sleeping people. They left the gallery and came to a flight of stone steps going down.

"I don't remember seeing those steps on the museum map," said Kirsty. "I wonder what's down there."

"Let's find out," said Rachel.

They shone their torches down the steps and Rachel led the way. The air got colder.

"I think this must be an old part of the museum," said Kirsty, shining her torch around. "The walls look as if they belong in a castle."

At the bottom of the steps, there was a long gallery.

"It's completely empty," said Kirsty. "That's strange."

They shone their torches around. The walls were bare, and there were no displays.

"Kirsty, look at your torch," exclaimed Rachel. "It's sparkling."

"Oh my goodness," said Kirsty.

The end of her torch unscrewed itself, but the light didn't go out. It got brighter. Rachel and Kirsty shared an excited smile. They had seen this kind of light before. To their delight, a tiny, red-haired

fairy spiralled out of the torch. She was wearing a simple T-shirt and jeans, with an orange neck scarf and a long, brown coat.

"It's Annie the Detective Fairy," said Rachel. "Hello, Annie!"

Annie waved at them and flicked her wand. Kirsty's torch instantly mended itself.

"It's great to see you," said Rachel. "Do you know what this place is?"

Annie looked around.

"It's the oldest gallery in the museum," she said. "It was built here two hundred years ago by a famous engineer. The very first exhibition was all about astronomy. It showed some of the most exciting inventions for studying the stars and planets. But one day, all the displays disappeared."

"Were they stolen?" asked Kirsty.

"That's the mystery," said Annie. "Even the cabinets and the tables vanished. I don't think burglars would have taken those."

"Couldn't you find out by looking in the queen's Seeing Pool?" Rachel asked.

Annie's eyes sparkled.

"I might be able to do that," she said. "But it's no fun solving mysteries that way. Detectives work things out for themselves ... with a little bit of luck, of course. One day, I feel sure that someone will solve the mystery of the missing displays."

"In the meantime, we need to solve the mystery of the missing notebooks," said Kirsty. "What could Jack Frost be doing with them?"

"I can show you exactly what he's doing with mine," said Annie. "Orla the Inventor Fairy spotted him with her scanner this morning. Will you come to Fairyland and help me to get my notebook back? It helps all detectives to keep thinking clearly. But as long as Jack Frost has it, their thoughts will be muddled and they won't be able to solve their cases."

"We'll come," Rachel and Kirsty said together.

Annie twirled her wand and then pointed it towards the girls. A bright ribbon of sparkling fairy dust coiled out

of it. Then the ribbon changed shape.

"It's turning into a magnifying glass," said Rachel.

The fairy-dust magnifying glass hung in the air. It shone a glimmering light on the girls, and they felt themselves shrinking to fairy size.

Chapter Two
Hello Fairyland!

Rachel and Kirsty's delicate wings
opened like petals. The magnifying glass
faded away, and the three fairies shared a
hug.

"Goodness, this gallery looks even
bigger now," said Kirsty with a laugh.

"I love being a fairy," said Rachel,

fluttering across to the nearest wall. "Fairies can see things that human eyes don't spot."

She hovered beside a small hole in the wall.

"I can see a metal loop in there," said Kirsty, coming to peer into the hole. "Let's pull it and see what happens."

The fairies reached into the hole and tugged on the metal loop.

"Goodness, it's stiff," said Kirsty. "I don't think we're strong enough."

"Let's try it when we're human again," said Rachel. "Right now I think we're needed in Fairyland."

Eager to help their friends, Rachel and Kirsty watched as Annie waved her wand. The walls around them seemed to melt away into thousands of twinkling stars.

"They're beautiful," said Kirsty, reaching out her arms.

The stars spun faster and faster.

"It's like being on a fairground ride," said Rachel, laughing. "I'm dizzy."

She closed her eyes, and then felt warm sunlight on her face. Before she opened her eyes, she smiled.

"Hello, Fairyland," she whispered.

They were standing in the middle of an almost-perfect circle of five toadstool houses. Where the sixth house should have been, there was only a round patch of bare earth.

"What sweet houses," said Kirsty. "But there's one missing."

"Yes," said Annie. "Without the sixth house, it isn't a real fairy ring."

"I've seen those in the fields around

Wetherbury," said Rachel. "They're big circles of mushrooms."

Annie nodded.

"There are lots of human myths and legends about fairy rings," she said. "Some people believe that they appear wherever fairies have danced in a circle."

"But really they are fairy homes," said Rachel, smiling.

She had always loved the toadstool houses that were dotted all over Fairyland's green hills.

"There's something strange about these houses," said Kirsty. "There are no curtains in the windows."

"And there are weeds growing in the gardens," said Rachel in surprise.

"That's because no one has lived in these houses for a very long time," said Annie. "It's all because of Fairyland's oldest mystery."

Rachel and Kirsty tingled with curiosity.

"Why have you brought us here?" Kirsty asked.

Just then, the door of the house opposite opened. Kirsty jumped, and Rachel gave a cry of alarm. Jack Frost was standing in

the doorway!

"It's OK," said Annie in a glum voice. "He's not here to cause trouble."

"Then why is he here?" asked Rachel. "And why is he wearing those clothes?"

Jack Frost had swapped his usual blue cloak for a very old-fashioned outfit. He had a thick coat with a little cape and a matching hat with earflaps.

Behind him was a small goblin, who

was also strangely dressed. He was
wearing a brown suit and a black hat,
and carrying a black doctor's bag. The
most surprising thing of all was the
wonky white beard that was stuck to his
chin.

"He's investigating," said Annie. "He
says that he's not called Jack Frost any
more. His name is Shivershock Bones,
and that goblin with him is Dr Gobson.
That's why I said they're not here to
cause trouble. They're trying to solve a
mystery."

"I understand now," said Kirsty, stifling
a giggle. "He's pretending to be Sherlock
Holmes."

"Yes," said Annie. "Sherlock Holmes
was one of the greatest and most
famous storybook detectives of all time.

25

Together with his
friend Dr Watson, he
solved hundreds of
mysteries. He used his
clever brain and his
powers of deduction.
But Shivershock Bones doesn't want to
spend time thinking and working things
out. He's using my magical notebook and
he thinks it will make him the greatest
detective ever."

"Quiet, pesky fairy!" commanded
Shivershock Bones.

He held up a magnifying glass and
glared at her through it.

"Oh no, there are three of them," he
went on.

"What are they doing here?" the goblin
asked.

"Easy-peasy, my dear Gobson," said Shivershock Bones. "They've come to take my magical notebook. But they can't have it!"

Dr Gobson sniggered and blew a raspberry at the fairies. Annie shook her head.

"As long as he has my magical notebook, detectives won't be able to solve their cases," she said. "We have to

get it back."

"We will," said Rachel, taking a step forward. "Excuse me, er, Shivershock Bones?"

"Go away," he snapped, glaring at her. "My amazing brain is busy thinking."

"Thinking about what?" Rachel asked.

Shivershock Bones didn't reply. He clasped his hands behind his back and started pacing up and down. Mr Gobson scurried along beside him.

"I'll explain," said Annie. "Jack Frost stole my magical notebook to turn himself into the greatest detective ever. He thinks that he can solve Fairyland's oldest mystery. That's why he's here."

"But what is the oldest mystery in Fairyland?" asked Kirsty.

Chapter Three
The Mystery of the Missing Toadstool

Annie sat down cross-legged in the middle of the circle, and Rachel and Kirsty did the same.

"The story begins a long time ago," said Annie. "A group of six fairy friends asked the very first queen of Fairyland for new homes. She used her magic to

create a ring of six toadstool houses
around a sparkling pond. It was a
beautiful place. The gardens were filled
with flowers, and the windows sparkled
in the sunshine. The friends were happy."

Kirsty glanced around.

"There's no pond here now," she said.
"And the gardens look wild. What
happened?"

"No one knows," said Annie. "One day,
all six fairies vanished and were never
seen again. One of the toadstool houses
vanished too, as well as the sparkling
pond. The queen looked everywhere, but
even the Seeing Pool couldn't help. They
had simply disappeared."

Rachel and Kirsty gasped.

"Many fairies have tried to solve the
mystery, but all have failed," said Annie.

"I have always dreamed that one day, I would find out the truth."

"I'm sure if anyone can solve the case, it'll be you," said Kirsty. "Are there any clues?"

"Yes, there were two clues," said Annie.

"The first clue was balloons. Where the missing toadstool house had been, there were six coloured balloons tied to a post in the ground."

There was an unpleasant cackle of laughter behind them. They looked around and saw Shivershock Bones and Dr Gobson.

"Balloons aren't clues," scoffed Shivershock Bones.

"Anything can be a clue," said Annie. "Good detectives notice everything."

"Give Annie's notebook back," said Rachel, springing to her feet. "You're

spoiling things for detectives all over the world."

"I don't care about them," said Shivershock Bones, curling his lip. "I only care about marvellous me, me, ME!"

Kirsty was still thinking about the balloons.

"There must have been a party," she said.

Everyone, even Shivershock Bones, turned to look at her.

"Yes," said Annie. "We think that the balloons had been outside the toadstool house to show where the party was."

"A party?" said Shivershock Bones, frowning. "I've never heard that bit of the story before."

"That's because you don't listen to anyone except yourself," said Dr Gobson.

Shivershock Bones ignored him.

"A party … and a toadstool house … and fairies," he muttered. "That reminds me of something."

Kirsty stood up and turned to Annie.

"You told us that there were two clues," she said. "What was the second one?"

"A shape," said Annie. "Where the pond had been, the grass was flattened into a special shape."

"What shape?" Shivershock Bones demanded. "I never heard about that either. Why didn't someone tell me?"

"Stop shouting," said Dr Gobson, putting his hands over his pointy ears.

"It's fairy history," said Annie. "You have never been interested in learning about us. You're usually too busy trying to spoil things."

34

"What shape?" Shivershock Bones yelled.

Annie didn't reply.

"Perhaps you should try saying 'please'," Rachel suggested.

Shivershock Bones's eyes looked as if they were going to pop out of his head. His face turned deep purple. Through gritted teeth, he hissed a single word.

"Please."

"It was the shape of a goblin footprint," said Annie.

Dr Gobson's mouth fell open. He gawped at Annie.

"A goblin footprint," Shivershock Bones said, starting to pace up and down again. "A goblin footprint."

"Er, Mr Frost?" said the goblin.

"Shut up!" Shivershock Bones yelled.

"Not another word. I'm thinking!"

Suddenly he clapped his hands together and laughed.

"Yes!" he shouted. "I'm sure I've heard something about fairies and balloons before, when I was no bigger than an icicle. An old family story …"

"What do you mean?" asked Rachel.

"None of your business," said Shivershock Bones. "Come on, Dr Gobson. We're going to search my castle from top to bottom until we find the answer. And fairies aren't invited!"

With a loud crack and a flash of blue lightning, Shivershock Bones and Dr Gobson vanished.

Chapter Four
Clients for Shivershock Bones

Rachel and Kirsty whirled around to face Annie.

"He knows something!" cried Rachel.

"We have to get into the Ice Castle somehow," said Kirsty.

Annie was breathless with excitement.

"I agree," she said. "I think the goblin

knows something too. Did you see
his face when I mentioned the goblin
footprint?"

Rachel and Kirsty nodded, their hearts
hammering.

"Jack Frost said something about an
old family story," said Rachel. "Maybe
his family had something to do with the
fairies disappearing."

"These are really good clues," said
Annie. "I wish my thoughts weren't so
muddled. I feel as if I could work it all
out if I had my magical notebook."

"That's another reason for us to go to
the Ice Castle," said Kirsty. "I bet that's
where your magical notebook is hidden.
Come on, Rachel and Annie. There's no
time to lose!"

The three fairies streaked into the air

and zoomed towards the coldest corner of Fairyland. The sky turned grey and the air grew chilly as they flew. Soon they saw the Ice Castle ahead. It looked chillier and more miserable than ever.

"There are more bars on the windows," said Rachel. "We won't be able to get in that way."

They landed on the sill of one of the tower windows. There was no one inside the room, but furious yells were echoing around the tower.

"I know it's a spell, you blithering blockhead!" an angry voice was shouting. "But what sort of spell? And why would my great-great-grandfather have it?"

"It sounds as if he's found a clue," said Rachel.

"Maybe you should ask the detective

41

fairy," said a trembling goblin voice.

"I'm not asking a pesky fairy for help!" roared the Ice Lord. "Fetch me her magical notebook. The answer will come to me if I'm holding that!"

Annie shook the bars of the window.

"I have to get in there," she cried. "Until my magical notebook is back

where it belongs, no detective anywhere will be able to think clearly."

"And I want to see that clue," said Kirsty. "I've got a feeling that we might really have a chance to solve this mystery."

"I've got an idea," said Rachel. "The real Sherlock Holmes always had mysterious clients arriving at his home to ask for his help. Let's knock on the castle door and say that we are clients."

"Brilliant idea," said Annie, clapping her hands together. "Jack Frost will be so curious, he'll have to see us!"

They fluttered down to the door, and then Annie waved her wand. At once, each fairy was wearing a long cloak and a veil.

"No one would recognise us," said

Kirsty. "What brilliant disguises."

Rachel raised her hand to the door.

KNOCK! KNOCK! KNOCK!

The three fairies held their breath as the sound rang out. From inside the castle, they could hear scurrying footsteps. Then the oak door opened a crack. A long nose poked out, attached to a grumpy goblin face.

"What?" he barked.

"We have come to see Jack — er, I mean — Shivershock Bones," said Kirsty in a loud voice. "We need his help."

The door slowly creaked open, and the fairies walked in. The goblin was wearing a white wig and a long black dress.

"I am the housekeeper," he said through gritted teeth. "Follow me."

He led them through the courtyard and up some tower steps. He kept tripping over his dress, and Rachel and Kirsty had to try hard not to laugh. When they reached the door of the highest room in the tower, the goblin barged in.

"Clients," he squawked.

"Come in and meet the greatest detective in the world," said Shivershock Bones.

The goblin turned and left, pushing past the fairies as he went.

"I'm a guard, not a housekeeper," they heard him muttering.

Rachel, Kirsty and Annie walked into the room. It was filled with ancient trunks, which all had their lids open.

Scrolls of paper covered the floor. Dr Gobson was half hidden under a pile of dusty books.

"Do you have a mystery for me to solve?" Shivershock Bones snapped.

"We need your help with a very confusing mystery indeed," said Rachel.

"We want to find a missing toadstool."

Shivershock Bones glared at them. "I am already working on that case," he said. "In fact, I have found a spell that holds the key to the whole mystery."

He held up a torn, yellowing old piece

of paper. Spidery words were scrawled all over it.

"This is my great-great-grandfather's writing," he said.

Annie stepped forward and read the words.

"It's a vanishing spell for six fairies," she said. "This is it! Now we know what happened to the fairies. Your great-great-grandfather made them disappear. We could bring them back with the right spell. For them, no time would have passed."

"Just like when we go back to the human world," said Rachel.

"Oh my goodness," said Kirsty. "The mystery is solved."

Annie shook her head.

"Not quite," she said. "It doesn't explain

the missing toadstool, or the balloons,
or the mark on the ground. I want to
understand why he did it – and I want to
get my magical notebook back."

With a roar of anger, Shivershock
Bones snatched at Annie's veil. The cloak
slipped off her shoulders.

"Fairies!" he yelled.

Rachel and Kirsty took off their
disguises too.

"I'll lock you in the dungeons!"
Shivershock Bones bellowed. "I'll feed
you slug soup!"

"Nonsense," said Rachel in a firm
voice. "You won't do any such thing."

Chapter Five
The Pieces of the Puzzle

"What makes you think I won't make you my prisoners?" Shivershock Bones asked.

"You're too curious about the mystery," said Rachel. "If you lock us up, you'll never find out the truth."

"What do you mean?" asked Kirsty.

Rachel smiled.

"I have just realised that none of us will be able to solve this mystery alone," she said. "Each of us has a piece of the puzzle. We have to work as a team to find out the truth."

"You want me to work with fairies?" said Shivershock Bones. "Never!"

"With fairies and Dr Gobson," said Rachel, looking at the goblin. "I think he knows something."

Everyone stared at Dr Gobson, who started to tremble. Annie knelt down beside him and rested her hand on his arm.

"I know that Shivershock Bones didn't listen," she said in a gentle voice. "But we want to hear your story. Please, tell us what you know."

The bearded goblin took a deep breath.

"There's an old goblin tradition in my family," he said. "When you feel jealous of someone, you do something mean to them to get your own back. Then you leave a picture of your footprint to boast to other goblins about what you did."

"So that's why you looked so surprised when you heard about the goblin footprint on the grass," said Kirsty.

The goblin nodded.

"My great-great-grandmother always said that she once got her own back on six fairies at the same time," he said. "But no one ever believed her.

Maybe it was true!"

Everyone stared at the goblin for a moment. Then Shivershock Bones reached inside his coat and pulled out a faintly glowing purple notebook.

"This stupid thing isn't working properly," he said, glaring at it. "I still don't understand what happened."

"The notebook doesn't do your thinking for you," said Annie. "You still have to use your brain. But it does help you to think clearly."

Shivershock Bones thought for a moment. Then he held out the notebook to Annie.

"I think we've got all the clues," he said. "I want to know what happened all that time ago."

"Now we really are a team," said Annie.

She stood up and took the book. Its magical glow grew brighter as she tucked it under her arm. Annie blinked a few times and then tucked her hair behind her ears.

"That spell page was torn out of a book," she said in a brisk voice. "We must find that book."

They all got down on their knees

beside the piles of books. Even
Shivershock Bones joined in. One by one,
they checked each book. At last, Kirsty
gave a cry of excitement.

"I think this is it!" she said.

"That's my great-great-grandfather's
diary," said Shivershock Bones.

Annie waved her wand, and the torn

piece of paper fitted itself back into the book.

"What does it say before the spell?" she asked Kirsty.

Kirsty read aloud from the book.

"Today, a silly goblin came and asked me for a spell. She was jealous of some fairies with their new toadstool houses and their happy housewarming party. I told her that I would help, if she promised me that her family would work for my family for ever. The bird-brain agreed. Ha ha! Now I have servants to work for me and I've made six pesky fairies disappear. I am a genius!"

"That explains everything," said Annie.

"Including why the goblins work here," added Rachel.

"Those poor fairies," said Kirsty.

Annie smiled and her eyes sparkled.

"Now I know the whole story, I think I can break that old spell," she said.

Kirsty felt hope bubbling up inside her.

"Do you mean you can find the six fairies?" she asked. "Even after all this time?"

"We're a team, remember?" said Annie. "Shivershock Bones and Mr Gobson had some of the clues. The fairies knew about the balloons and the footprint shape. And you two asked all the right questions and had brilliant ideas."

"For once, we all worked together," said Rachel.

"Now we can go back to the toadstool houses and put things right," said Kirsty.

"Stop!" said Shivershock Bones in a

sharp voice.

The fairies
whirled around.
He was glaring
at them.

"I'm not letting
you bring those
fairies back," he
said. "That will break
the old deal, and the goblins won't do
what I say any more."

"You can't stop us," said Annie.

"We'll get out," said Kirsty.

Rachel was looking at Shivershock
Bones.

"We won't need to," she said in a quiet
voice. "Shivershock Bones likes being a
detective. He likes it enough to give back
the notebook. And real detectives never

Annie

stop until they get to the very end."

She crossed her fingers and hoped that she was right.

Chapter Six
Mystery Solved!

Shivershock Bones stared at Rachel for a few moments. Then, grumbling under his breath, he thumped his wand on the floor. There was a bright flash of blue light, and then they were all standing in the circle of toadstool houses.

Annie, Rachel and Kirsty shared a

happy smile. Then Annie raised her wand and spoke the words of a spell.

"Flip this Frosty spell around.
Return the toadstool to the ground.
Bring the fairies and the pond
Home to where they all belong."

For a moment, nothing happened. Then fairy magic started to twinkle in the air. The circle of toadstool houses glimmered with tiny stars. Then, in the empty space, another house appeared.

"It's see-through," said Rachel.

"Wait, it's getting more solid," said Kirsty.

"It's back," said Shivershock Bones.

The front door opened, and six fairies stood there, smiling at them.

"Hello," they said. "Are you here for the party?"

Annie, Rachel and Kirsty cheered and laughed, dancing around in delight. Dr Gobson gave a loud squawk. Even Shivershock Bones's mouth twitched.

While Annie went to explain to the

other fairies what had happened, Rachel and Kirsty turned to Shivershock Bones. He frowned.

"Are you going to carry on being a detective?" Kirsty asked.

"No way," he replied. "I'll never work with fairies again. I thought it would be fun to see the end of the mystery, but it's just annoying. I never want to hear the name Shivershock Bones again."

"The goblins are free!" squealed Dr Gobson. "Yippee!"

Jack Frost narrowed his eyes..

"You're not free," he said. "I have found an extra line in my great-great-grandfather's diary. The old goblin agreed that her family would work for my family for ever, even if the spell was broken."

"Is that true?" asked Rachel in astonishment.

Jack Frost didn't reply.

"Bother, bother, bother," grumbled Dr Gobson.

He stomped off in the direction of Jack Frost's Castle, and Jack Frost followed him, cackling. Rachel and Kirsty shared a happy smile as Annie fluttered over to them.

"It's time for me to send you home," she said. "I must return the magical notebook to Mission Control."

Rachel and Kirsty looked at the toadstool house. The six fairies were standing in the garden, smiling and waving.

"I wonder who they are and what they do," said Rachel.

"Maybe we should have a big party to welcome them home and get to know them," said Annie in an excited voice. "And you two should be the guests of honour. Without you, I wouldn't have solved anything."

"A party sounds wonderful," said Kirsty, hugging Annie. "We're just glad that you got a happy ending."

"Look out for your invitations very

soon," said Annie. "Thank you for all you did. Goodbye!"

In the blink of an eye, the girls were human again. They were back in the shadowy old gallery where the adventure had begun. Time always stood still in the human world when they went to Fairyland, so they knew that no one

would have missed them.

"Let's go and get some sleep," said
Kirsty. "I'm pretty tired after all that
detective work."

"Wait a minute," said Rachel.
"I promised myself that I would see

what that little hole was for, remember?"

She found the hole in the wall and pushed her little finger into it. She hooked another finger into the metal loops and pulled hard. It was stiff, but she didn't give up.

"It's coming," she said.

Suddenly, there was a loud scraping noise. It was the sound of stone moving across stone.

"Oh my goodness," said Kirsty. "The walls are moving!"

The girls watched in amazement. One by one, all four walls slid forwards, turned and then slid backwards again. But the new walls were not bare. They were

filled with pictures, cabinets and shelves.
There were telescopes of every shape and
size. There were tables with pulleys and
wheels, designs and models. Paintings

of stars and planets decorated the walls. Each display was old and incredible.

"They're a bit dusty," said Rachel with a grin. "But that makes sense, because I think these are the missing exhibits. Kirsty, these things are two hundred years old!"

Kirsty gasped in wonder at the amazing exhibits.

"So that's where they went," she said. "They were behind secret doors all these years. I wonder who hid them – and why."

"I can't wait to tell the museum staff," said Rachel.

She gave a huge yawn, and Kirsty laughed.

"We can tell them in the morning, and we'll think up a plan to get the

last magical notebook back too," she said. "But right now, we need to get some sleep. Just for tonight, we have an

extra secret. The mystery of the missing exhibition is solved!"

The End

**Now it's time for Kirsty and
Rachel to help ...**

Elsie the Engineer Fairy

Read on for a sneak peek ...

"Good morning, Rachel," said Kirsty
Tate.

Rachel Walker yawned, stretched and
opened her eyes. For a moment, she
couldn't think where she was. Then she
remembered, and sat up in her sleeping
bag feeling excited. She had spent the
night at the Science Museum sleepover,
and she had already shared three
amazing adventures with her best friend
Kirsty and the Discovery Fairies.

"Good morning," she said. "Is it time to
get up?"

Kirsty nodded. All around them,

children and grown-ups were yawning and crawling out of their sleeping bags. Mr Tate, who had come to the sleepover too, smiled at them.

"Let's go and find some breakfast," he said.

Still in their pyjamas, the girls rolled up their sleeping bags and followed Mr Tate to the far end of the Discover Space gallery. A table had been set up with bowls of cereal, fruit, toast and juice.

"Keep an eye out for Elsie the Engineer Fairy," Kirsty said in a low voice. "Jack Frost still has her magical notebook. I hope we can help her before it's time for us to go home."

The night before, the girls had met the Discovery Fairies and heard about their troubles. Jack Frost had stolen their precious magical notebooks. Without the notebooks, no one in the human or fairy worlds would be able to make new discoveries. They had managed to find three of the notebooks, but one was still missing.

"We need to tell the museum staff about the hidden gallery we found," Rachel remembered.

During their midnight adventure, the girls had found a secret room full of long-lost exhibits.

"Yes, but let's have some breakfast first," said Kirsty. "My tummy's rumbling."

As they were finishing their food, a young man in museum uniform hurried into the gallery.

"Good morning, everyone!" he said. "I'm Ben, and I'll be your guide this morning. I hope you slept well, and had a wonderful evening! Before you all go home, we have one last discovery for you. Please follow me."

Feeling excited, the group from the Discover Space gallery followed him through long corridors and up a flight of steps. At the top, they saw a big sign.

Read **Elsie the Engineer Fairy** to find out what adventures are in store for Kirsty and Rachel!

RAINBOW magic

Calling all parents, carers and teachers!
The Rainbow Magic fairies are here to help
your child enter the magical world of reading.
Whatever reading stage they are at, there's
a Rainbow Magic book for everyone!
Here is Lydia the Reading Fairy's guide to
supporting your child's journey at all levels.

Starting Out

Our Rainbow Magic Beginner Readers are perfect for first-time readers who are just beginning to develop reading skills and confidence. Approved by teachers, they contain a full range of educational levelling, as well as lively full-colour illustrations.

Developing Readers

Rainbow Magic Early Readers contain longer stories and wider vocabulary for building stamina and growing confidence. These are adaptations of our most popular Rainbow Magic stories, specially developed for younger readers in conjunction with an Early Years reading consultant, with full-colour illustrations.

Going Solo

The Rainbow Magic chapter books - a mixture of series and one-off specials - contain accessible writing to encourage your child to venture into reading independently. These highly collectible and much-loved magical stories inspire a love of reading to last a lifetime.

www.rainbowmagicbooks.co.uk

"Rainbow Magic got my daughter reading chapter books. Great sparkly covers, cute fairies and traditional stories full of magic that she found impossible to put down" - Mother of Edie (6 years)

"Florence LOVES the Rainbow Magic books. She really enjoys reading now" - Mother of Florence (6 years)

The Rainbow Magic
Reading Challenge

Well done, fairy friend – you have completed the book!
This book was worth 5 points.

See how far you have climbed on the
Reading Rainbow opposite.

The more books you read, the more points you will get,
and the closer you will be to becoming a Fairy Princess!

How to get your Reading Rainbow
1. Cut out the coin below
2. Go to the Rainbow Magic website
3. Download and print out your poster
4. Add your coin and climb up the Reading Rainbow!

There's all this and lots more at
www.rainbowmagicbooks.co.uk

You'll find activities, competitions, stories, a special
newsletter and complete profiles of all the
Rainbow Magic fairies. Find a fairy with your name!